Barris
and the
Girl of Norizon

WRITTEN BY

Brandt Ricca

ILLUSTRATED BY

Matt Miller

Ricca, Brandt. *Barris and the Girl of Norizon.*

Copyright © 2022 by Brandt Ricca

Illustrations by Matt Miller

Cover layout and book design by Liona Design Co., www.lionadesignco.com

Published by KWE Publishing: www.kwepub.com

ISBN (hardback): 979-8-9853464-4-2
ISBN (paperback): 979-8-9853464-5-9
ISBN (ebook): 979-8-9853464-6-6

Library of Congress Control Number: 2022905370

Acknowledgements

Brandt and Matt would like to thank those who have been instrumental in the *Barris Books* series. Without them, and their belief in dreams and imagination, none of this would be possible.

Kim Eley, Crystal Cregge, Adriane Miller, Brian Winterfeldt and the Winterfeldt IP team, Caity Byrne, Candice Wright, Jonathan Thorpe, Michael Akin & the LINK team, Mita Moody & The Four Seasons Hotel-Georgetown.

...and last but not least, all of their friends and family.

Table des Matières

Dedication

"To my Aunt Robin. A woman who's imagination and awakening conversations always leaves me curious about the world."

— BRANDT RICCA, AUTHOR

"To my husband, Bryan, for being forever loving and endlessly supportive."

— MATT MILLER, ILLUSTRATOR

1

____

Chapitre Un...

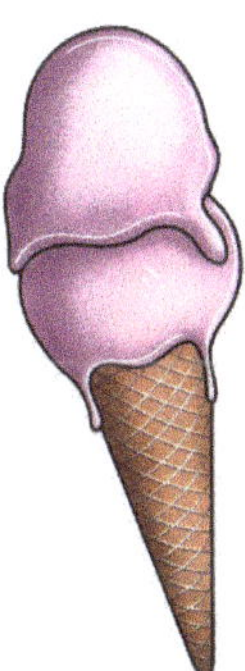

"Let's go somewhere." Pevy said while she gazed across the street at a couple that looked to be in love, giggling, holding hands. They appeared to be in an enchanted state. A trumpet player stood a few feet away from the couple, playing a tune. His hat sat on the ground and had crumpled up dollar bills in it. His melody provided a soundtrack for the young couple nearby.

Barris, Glenda, Dean and Pevy all sat on a street bench outside Schwegmann's Grocery on Burgundy Street on a mild New Orleans Sunday afternoon.

It was Spring Break 1953. They were eating ice cream cones, licking the delicious sherbert flavor while it dripped down their fingers.

"Where do you want to go?" Barris asked, turning the cone to catch the drips on his tongue. He wore his favorite blue hat.

"Somewhere. Somewhere where the only thing to keep you company is the sky, the trees and the stars," Pevy said, in a dreamlike state.

"Isn't that just a field?" Glenda asked, laughing and wiping her hands on her purple overalls. She wore the overalls all the time.

"Don't you ever wash those?" Dean had asked once.

"Yes of course, but I have five pairs, and they fit me perfectly," Glenda had said. "And a girl my size hangs onto an outfit that suits her."

Pevy looked up at Glenda while they sat on the bench. Glenda was so much bigger than the rest of them. Pevy felt an overwhelming sense of being misunderstood by her friends.

Spring break for children is normally a happy time. A break from school, time to eat sweets, play in the streets and to sleep in. Well…for other kids at least. Pevy was being sent to charm school during her break. She had been misbehaving at home.

I, Gracie, being a Keeper of the Universe, am privy to everything in a child's reality but only able to communicate with them while they slumber in their dream worlds, and help guide them through. I leaned against a brick wall across the street, while eavesdropping on Barris and his friends. Of course, I was enjoying a cold treat myself. "Treats for everyone!" I shouted out loud as I opened my arms to the world. I knew no one could hear me.

Pevy had been acting out recently because her parents were separating. Over the last two years her parents, Mr. and Mrs. Wollendrop, had grown distant. They became "passing ships in the night" when they were home. And they seemed to be different people and would fight over the smallest everyday things.

Mr. Wollendrop traveled a lot for work. He was rarely home, and Mrs. Wollendrop fancied herself a flirt every time she encountered anyone, whether it be the milk man or the little old lady she ran into at Schwegmann's Grocery. Her demeanor was that of someone who had lived multiple lives, like she knew the secret to life, and wanted to embrace each person she passed.

Mrs. Wollendrop would wear the tightest dresses she could squeeze into and kept her hair teased in a bouffant. Her brown shoulder-length hair flipped up at the bottom, just above her collar. She looked at every moment outside the house as an opportunity for something grand to happen, and she would most certainly be dressed for it. High heels and big sunglasses accompanied her red-colored mouth and a headscarf, her hair's constant accessory to keep the wind from messing it up.

Barris would sometimes overhear his mom, Mrs. Hart, and Glenda's mom, Mrs. Longthistle, describe Pevy's mom as a woman with "loose morals." Whatever that meant, Barris had no idea. The other mothers would just stare with widened eyes when she walked by. While the younger girls would see her and tell Pevy, "Your mom is such a Betty," Pevy would roll her eyes each time out of embarrassment.

Mr. Wollendrop was going out of town for a month on business to California. Before he left, he and his wife sat with Pevy to let her know that they would be separating upon his return. Pevy wasn't surprised at all by the news, but the words still knocked the wind out of her body. She sat on her hands and listened in her tiny yellow shotgun house on Royal Street.

She felt one of the buttons on the seat of the tufted leather couch where she sat. She could hear her parents talking to her. It was hard to understand what they were saying. She pulled on the button to distract herself. Her eyes focused on the light blue wall behind her parents, to a picture hanging there.

It was of the three of them, and their dog Charlotte. A timid, anxious terrier mix. It was the day they had adopted the dog as a puppy. Pevy looked so happy as she bent down to Charlotte's height, and her parents stood above her laughing in the framed memory that hung on one medium-sized rusty nail. "Isn't that perfect?" Pevy thought while she stared at the rust. Her gaze then turned to her father's suitcase by the door. A common occurrence due to his work travel, but this time...it was different.

• •

That was three weeks ago. Since then, Pevy had started talking back to her mother regularly, while they were home without her father.

"You ruin everything!" Pevy shouted one evening as she stomped down the hall to her room. "You didn't even try!" While Pevy would only ever admit to herself that it was more peaceful in the house with the decision her parents had made, she didn't view them as individual human beings. She viewed her parents as a unit, a block that was sold at a "two for one special." Having recently turned ten years old, Pevy would look back on that time years later and know that it was the right decision her parents made.

While Pevy screamed, stomped and slammed doors, her mother would say, "Pevania Wollendrop! Don't make me come up there." They both knew she wouldn't budge. She would then let out a loud exhale while reading *LIFE* magazine. On the cover of that particular issue was "America's First Family." Well at least for that moment. It was Lucille Ball and Desi Arnaz, with their two children. They had a very popular and funny TV show at that time, "I Love Lucy." For people like Pevy and Mrs. Wollendrop who felt lonely at home, the show was an escape, a chance to laugh. A temporary story that was different from their reality.

Often people get lost in stories, even if they're ones they tell themselves.

While Pevy sat on the bench with her friends outside of Schwegmann's, all they knew was that she was being sent to *Madame Sylvie's Charm School for Girls*, and that she was in trouble at home. Her friends were unaware that she was in trouble at home as a response to her parent's separation. She was too embarrassed to tell them that detail. At least for now.

"Pevy you'll sure be missed this week while we build our treehouse," Barris said.

Pevy was to start at Madame Sylvie's the following Monday morning.

"We are going to make it big enough for ALL of us to fit into it," Glenda assured the group. She felt she always needed to make them aware that she needed to have room too, in whatever they did.

After their small indulgence outside of Schwegmann's, Barris and his friends retreated to their respective homes for dinner.

Barris rode his new Schwinn red bicycle that he had just gotten. It was his "big boy" bike, as his mother would say.

He cruised to the tall staircase that went up the middle of his tall green house, hopped off and let the bike fall to the ground. He couldn't be bothered to put the kick stand down. "So lazy," I thought as I watched him.

The sun was setting on Frenchmen Street, and so were the busy lives of all its inhabitants.

"Bonjour mon fils!" Mrs. Hart exclaimed when she heard their front door close. She was rushing around the kitchen to the sounds of her beloved Ella. (That would be Ella Fitzgerald, her favorite jazz singer.) After Mrs. Hart's exclamation, Barris heard his tone-deaf mother singing along, "Another season, another reason, for makin' whoopee!"

Mrs. Hart sang and hummed while she brought dishes of her latest French cuisine to the dinner table. Barris walked into his living room to plop down on the couch. His sister Bernice was lying on the floor reading a book. Bernice considered herself a simple gal and loved lying on the living room floor. She would read, watch TV or simply relax. Mrs. Hart would force her to sit in actual furniture whenever they had company over.

"Boeuf bourguignon!" Francine Hart exclaimed to herself with a French accent thrown on each sound, while she tossed salt on the dish. She was very proud of the dinner she made that evening. It meant "beef Burgundy," which is a beef stew made in red wine.

"Dîner est servi!" (Dinner is served!)

2

Chapitre Deux...

"Nightmare Child!" Madame Sylvie shouted to Pevy on that Monday afternoon. It was supposed to be her first day of Spring Break, but alas, there she was being subjected to "being a lady," "having manners" and "proper posture."

Madame Sylvie's Charm School for Girls was in the French Quarter of New Orleans. It had a reputation for producing the "South's Southern Lady." Or at least that was the advertisement Pevy's mother had shown her before she sent her there. Her school looked like a typical New Orleans house, was bright pink with wooden chairs and fluffy cushions decorating the porch.

Madame Sylvie was from Paris, France and had moved to New Orleans a few years prior. She was a skinny woman who wore black pencil skirts, multiple pearl necklaces around her neck and oversized white silk shirts with ruffles. You could hear her coming from anywhere, as she marched

about in black high heels, always on a mission. She was a curious woman. You didn't know whether to be suspicious of her or enchanted by her.

Behind her was her lowly assistant, Anastasia (ANA-STAHSH-YA). Each time the Madame said her name she ended with a high pitched "Ya!" She skittered frantically behind her employer, carrying papers and a notebook, scribbling notes for what the Madame needed.

"Anastasia, this one needs a hair trim. This one needs new clothes. This one needs..." She would say sternly, with her heavy French accent. The Madame was constantly playing with the pearls on her neck, while judging her new students, looking them up and down.

Standing there on her first day with the group of other new girls, "the new batch," Madame Sylvie called them, Pevy could feel herself start to sweat as Madame edged closer. With each girl, a new insult.

Pevy looked at the ground. When she saw the two black high heels stand in front of her, she followed the line of her stockings, skirt and ruffles. Pevy's eyes met the Madame's. They stood there in complete silence for thirty seconds. One glare so anxious, the other so adamant of her mission.

Looking Pevy up and down, Madame Sylvie tousled her pearl necklaces, then paused holding on to them. Behind her, Anastasia waited with her pencil poised next to "Pevania Wollendrop."

"Ce n'est pas terrible," she stated. "Will need quite the makeover. Let's make her look like a lady, shall we?

• •

Hmmm?" She nodded "Oui?" to Pevy.

Surrounding the new girls within the charm school were photos of all the Madame's successes. Girls when they entered and left as ladies. Bangs curled, lashes twirled and their spines straight.

Over the course of the next few days, Pevy would spend her time walking in straight lines while balancing a book on her head, learning how to sit properly with her knees angled just so, whether at a dinner or social gathering. And more importantly, she would learn how to exude an air of elegance.

The week or the days didn't seem so bad to Pevy. She in fact didn't mind the strict atmosphere of the new learning so much. Madame Sylvie's teachings were a great distraction from what was going on at home.

On Thursday after charm school, Pevy met Barris, Glenda and Dean in front of Barris' house to go bike riding. "You're it!" Dean slapped Pevy's arm and sped off on his bright yellow Schwinn bicycle. Schwinn bicycles were the "it" thing to have in the neighborhoods among the kids that year.

Pevy had been staring at the sky and had just come off a long day of "lady learning" and had to readjust to her usual playful self with her friends. She kicked her foot off the ground and stood up on her pedals to put the weight into each push with her feet. Dean and Glenda had sped ahead to avoid getting tagged.

While riding his red bicycle, Barris was adjusting his pack. It was the pack that Papaw Leo had given him so he'd always feel prepared for anything. He didn't see his grandfather much anymore, who was living in a nice building in upstate New York, with a staff of people seeing to his every whim. "He seems better," Barris' dad would say.

Since he was playing with his pack, Barris wasn't going as fast as Dean and Glenda up ahead.

"You're going to get tagged," I thought about Barris as I leapt next to them. It was as if my shoes had Slinkys built into them.

I love to check in on my assigned children often. Being aware of what is going on in their realities helps me help them in their dream worlds.

"You're it," Pevy said when she slowly swatted Barris' hand. After she tagged him, she stayed next to him, coasting on her bike.

"I feel like something's wrong," Barris said to her, while he coasted alongside. "You've been different lately." He didn't bother trying to tag her again. "Dean said he saw you yelling at your mother on your porch the other day."

"If I tell you something, do you pinkie swear to not say anything to anyone?" Pevy asked anxiously. "I promise." Barris responded.

"I mean it, Barris Hart!" She didn't say it for him; she had to reiterate it again for herself.

She then rolled on her bike next to her friend and retold the tale of that day on the leather couch, within the blue walls, in her yellow house. The day where she was surrounded by moments of her happy family that hung on the walls. Being told a new chapter was about to begin in her life. A story of a broken home.

Barris didn't know how to react. He had never heard of someone's parents separating. He had never heard of parents leading separate lives. And he most certainly had never heard of a child having to go visit two homes, with a parent at each.

He became uncomfortable hearing the sad story from his friend. This was new territory, and when something is new territory for someone and they don't understand it, they can become uneasy and sometimes shut down.

"It's just like she doesn't care," Pevy said about her mother, as Barris tried to navigate the thoughts that swirled in his head. She was about to tell Barris of their latest fight when Barris interrupted her.

"I think my mom said I could only come out for a few minutes. I gotta jet, but I'll see you later this week after you complete Madame Sylvie's, ok?" He threw a faint smile at her.

He did a U-turn in the street and was going so fast he almost toppled over on his bicycle. He pedaled as fast as he could for the two blocks to his house. He never looked behind him; he just wanted to get out of sight from Pevy and get back to comfort behind the front door of his house. Where his home was still the same. The life he knew.

Pevy took a deep breath...and then another. Being at charm school for a few days had already crept into her. She knew how to maintain her composure. She waited for a few moments as her feet stood on either side of her bicycle. The sounds of *"C'est Si Bon"* by Eartha Kitt wafted from a kitchen window. Pevy batted at her hair with both hands, and then started to pedal to try to catch up to Dean and Glenda. The horns from the nearby song blared as she rode away.

I stood in the street. I looked to my left towards Barris' house, then looked to my right to see Pevy pedaling off. Oh, how I wish I could talk to children when they are awake.

Later at the Hart residence, it was business as usual while the Hart children sat at their large dinner table. The warmth of the room and his mother humming brought comfort to Barris. He looked at Betsy and Betty, pre-teens who were gabbing about boys and what they would be doing with their friends the next day. Both had developed into what Barris would imagine Madame Sylvie would love. And he looked at Bernice, who was so uninterested in the twins or what they had to say. She licked her finger and turned the page of her latest read. Barris rolled his eyes when he saw her do that.

And then he looked at his parents. Mr. and Mrs. Hart. "Oh, fiddle dee dee, fiddle dee la la la," Mrs. Hart would sing while bringing dinner to the table or doing things around the house. When she sang, Mr. Hart was her biggest fan. Their fingers would touch whenever they walked past each other. Their encounters always seemed to happen in slow motion, whether it was the fingers touching in passing, or Mr. Hart twirling Mrs. Hart in the kitchen as she cooked. Those encounters showed the Hart children what love looked like. The "magic," Mrs. Hart would call it.

"Come and give me some of that magic," she would exclaim to the children for hugs and kisses everyday.

Throughout the world, there are many forms of love, Grandma Lucy would tell me. But the best form of love is the kind that feels surreal, like home…like "magic," to quote Mrs. Hart. Love is a mix of wild feelings. Grandma Lucy was the greatest Keeper of children's dreams, and always wise with her observations. If she were still with us, she'd be standing next to me, I have no doubt, and telling me how much she loves Mrs. Hart. Their personalities were similar. Everything they touched vibrated warmth.

As Barris observed his fortunate family, his blue eyes went from one member to the next, around the table. Smiling to himself at their quirks, he had a newfound sense of gratitude. "Could this all change?" he thought. He thought of Pevy and how he didn't know how to react to her news. How the existence she knew, an existence he thought was similar to his, was now foreign.

After dinner, Barris was in bed with heavy eyes, tired from a day of playing outside. A couple days left of Spring Break, then back to the normal school routine Monday.

When he closed his eyes, he heard the giggles of Mr. and Mrs. Hart who were slow dancing in the living room below to "Ella." He smiled, hearing the familiar nightly sounds.

A saxophone player from a block away provided tunes for passersby. The notes from the saxophone floated through the sky, through the Hart's tall green house, and through the walls of Barris' room. A "D" note scooped

• •

Barris up and out of his bedroom window. Children enter their dream worlds based on their surroundings. Barris was always scooped up by the musical notes of the neighboring streets. That night he was floating high, and felt he was floating on more than music.

3

Chapitre Trois...

Snowflakes fell, and then melted on Barris' face. He opened his eyes and blinked a few times for his eyes to focus.

He stood up to brush away the layer of snow that covered his blue and white striped pajamas, adjusted the pack around his waist and pulled down his blue hat snug against his head.

Behind him was nothing but blackness. He couldn't see walls, light or any features. Ahead of him was a snow-covered path. He thought for a moment, but knew he should go with what lay before him.

He was expecting to run into me almost right away, as he usually did. But I would not be with Barris in that world, on that night.

He walked ahead and with each step, he created a footprint in the snow. He was a little chilly, and his breath appeared before his face. The snow fell slower than snow could ever fall. With a few steps the snow faded away, and green grass was sprouting around Barris. Flowers and butterflies began to appear. Then the sun came out, and shined as brightly as the sun could shine. Now Barris was warm. He unbuttoned the top buttons on his pajama shirt, then realized he'd need to button them again. A fresh breeze cooled him. And the bright green leaves of the trees then turned to gold and started to fall around him like sprinkles.

He was experiencing each season, in what felt like a matter of moments. Barris walked along the path, observing the changing seasons. But behind him, the view never changed. It was always black, no matter how far he walked. No sooner had he shuffled onto a big pile of brown and gold leaves, enjoying the crunching sound they made, did he look up.

Autumn leaves fell heavily in front of Barris' face and he couldn't see for a moment, then they cleared and he was able to see what was before him. It was unlike any dream world he had been in before.

Drapery hung like sheets billowing on a laundry line. Shades of blue, red, purple and yellow, sometimes fading into green. It looked like the colors of the rainbow. They all cascaded down the front of a large brown building, floating in the air and attached to nothing.

The building was in the middle of a large, wide tunnel that went as high as Barris could see. Nothing else was around. Barris grabbed an edge of the drapery and moved it out of the way. An illuminating door stood ajar before him, and Barris walked through. Inside the interior walls were covered with what looked like fancy wallpaper. Deep burgundy colors with golden trim moved and shifted to different shapes and hues every few seconds. And the walls were three-dimensional. Barris thought he might be able to see through them, if it didn't make him so dizzy. It reminded him of a royal palace he'd seen in a book. Or an old Hollywood hotel he had seen in the movies.

In the middle of the large octagonal burgundy and gold room were floors, one above the other, that went up like a triangle, connected by stairs, but with no walls. Each floor became smaller than the one under it, and no top floor in sight. Endless platforms. There was a brass band sound off to the side that played fun, upbeat music, with horns, and instruments of all sorts. But...they were performing in the air as if by magic. No one was playing them. The instruments entertained hundreds of people surrounding Barris: people on each floor above him, around him, all moving with a sense of urgency. Then Barris realized he recognized the song they were playing. It was "Sing, Sing, Sing" by Benny Goodman. It was a song that Mr. and Mrs. Hart would dance to often. "Upbeat, fun, and an escape from reality," Mrs. Hart would say about the tune.

• •

This must be what it's like in New York City, he thought. He'd heard his Aunties and parents talk about it. Busy streets with hundreds of people, all walking intently.

Some people were flying around him, but they had no wings. Others were leaping, some extending their arms to grab something on another floor or at the end of the building. Each one of them carrying stacks and stacks of paper. He saw one person turn, and when they did, they became blurry and then they were somewhere else, walking up a staircase on the opposite side. Papers and the sounds of telephones ringing were everywhere. The glow of chandeliers, sconces and their Edison light bulbs provided a warm ambiance.

In the middle of this busyness and confusion was a man who kept walking up and down two sets of stairs, checking on papers or writing on different pages with a feathered pen. He reminded Barris of a concierge at a very busy hotel.

The man wore black and white striped socks, a gray trench coat that was closed tightly with a belt, and a green beret on his head. He looked very serious...and frantic. He didn't look at anything around him.

Barris moved to ask him where he was, and he then bumped into a little girl. All her papers flew up in the air, and fell just as slowly as the snowflakes had fallen when he woke up in that place.

"Hey! Watch where ya going!" the girl said to him. "Now help me!"

Barris thought she was me for a moment. She had my

facial features, black skin and purple eyes. The difference was she had a mole, a beauty mark next to her lip, and rather than red spaghetti hair, like mine, she had white spaghetti hair. And a black circular hat that she called her "crown." She wore green solid colored knee-high socks and black shoes. Her coat was brown, but different from the one I wore. It was not so large. Her belt that wrapped around her waist was orange, keeping her coat closed.

"I'm so sorry! I'm just looking around to see where I am."

"You don't know where you are? Who are you?" she questioned. "Help me, why don't you?" nodding at her papers, which were still falling. She was on her knees picking them up.

Barris knelt down to pick up some papers.

"I'm Barris, Barris Hart. And you?"

"I'm Lucille. And you, little boy, are not Barris, you are a distraction. You are distracting me. And you are in Norizon, by the way."

That night, when Barris had fallen asleep, he went back in time. He landed in dream headquarters, Norizon, where all Keepers live who monitor the dreams of sleeping children, until they are ten years old. That little girl was my Grandma Lucy, or "Lucille" as she used to call herself. Barris was meeting her at the age of nine, when she was just starting to be a Keeper herself.

Barris of course had heard of Norizon, and he knew that was where I hailed from, but he didn't realize he was with my Grandma Lucy.

• •

Barris wasn't my only assigned child, and on that night, I was with my newly assigned case, Bernice Hart. But that's a different tale, for a different time.

4

Chapitre Quatre...

Grelda was THE Universe witch. She had powers in all the dream worlds and Universes of sleeping children. She hailed from Dasa (DAH-SA) and also had power in Norizon. She was in charge of the training for all Keepers, and always has been. She never aged and has seen Norizon through many times.

Whenever Barris saw her, she would be wearing a purple dress that covered her feet, for no child can see her other than that way. But in Norizon, she wore a cape that was the color of sunset, and the cape draped in layers at her feet.

That night, I asked a favor of Grelda, to have Barris wake up back in time and get to know Grandma Lucy at that moment. Grelda would grant favors for Keepers sometimes, and in return they were to perform jobs for her when she needed them to. She was the dream Universe witch after all, and every bit of help she would take. On that night,

Barris would understand what goes into the business of dream-Keeping. Barris will be turning ten soon and then I won't be able to talk to him anymore when he slumbers. Grelda had obliged my wish.

But back to the busy, beautiful room, where papers were still drifting to the floor.

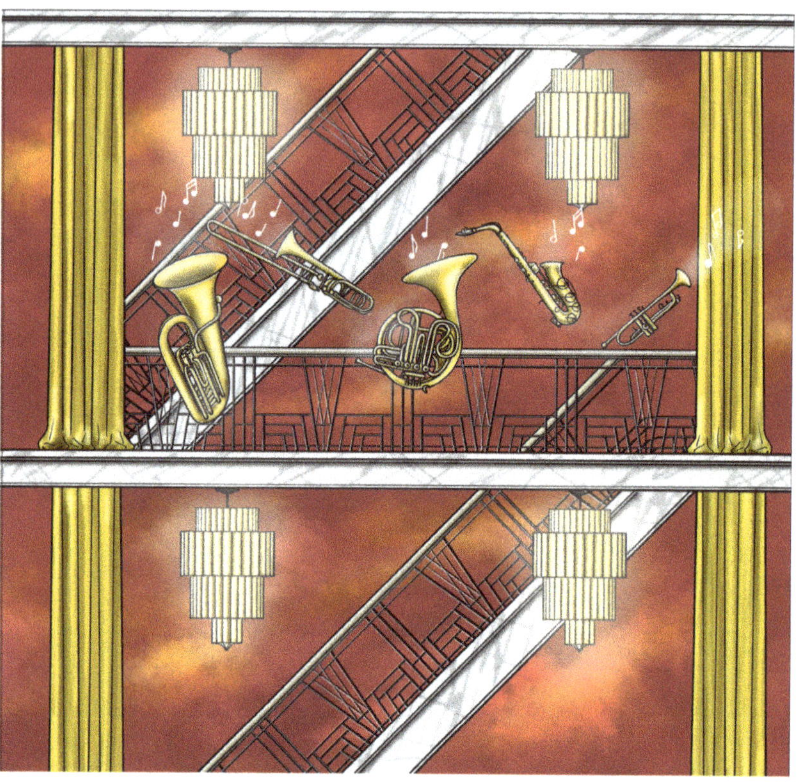

"I'm in Norizon?" Barris asked the little girl Lucille.

"That's what I said," she barked back.

Can you see where I got my personality from? Lucille of course.

"This is where Keepers live? You fix the dreams of children here?" Barris asked while he looked up at the busy Keepers, still hastily moving around them.

"Well, I'm trying to! Well…I'm about to. I'm about to graduate from Grelda's school. And then, don't worry children! I'll guide you!" she said, sweeping her arm up and behind her.

While Lucille and Barris collected the last of her drifting and fallen papers, a little boy approached.

"Luce! You're gonna be late!" he said to her.

"It's Lucille! I hate when you call me that." Lucille responded to the boy whom she clearly knew.

The little boy had dark brown skin and long black hair tied in a ponytail behind his head. His ponytail hung straight down to the middle of his back. He wore knee-high solid colored orange socks, a black trench coat and a yellow belt around his waist. On top of his head sat a yellow tweed newsboy hat. His eyes were purple, just like mine and Lucille's. All Keeper's have purple eyes. It's because their sight gives them insight.

Keepers in training wear solid colored socks and once they become a Keeper, they are given striped socks of their choosing.

"This is Neo," Lucille said to Barris. "He's about to be a Keeper too."

"I'm Barris."

"Delightful to meet you Barris. Are you in school too?

• •

I've never seen you before."

If Barris had learned anything from his dream worlds, it was to always go with the process of things. Which is actually the secret to life. Go with the flow of things, and not against them.

"First day!" Barris said and let out a little nervous laugh.

"That's definitely a different type of outfit for a Keeper in training," Neo said to him. He and Lucille looked Barris up and down and at his striped pajamas, hat and pack.

"I like to work lightly. This pack keeps all of my supplies, like the inside of your coats keep yours." Barris was remembering the inside of my jacket, always holding my things.

"Aces!" Lucille said.

"Aces?" Barris asked.

Lucille rolled her eyes, but smiled, "That means 'amazing,' silly."

"Oh, ok," Barris said. Everywhere he went there were new words and languages to adapt to.

As they stood there speaking, Barris began to feel a sense of urgency, as if he needed to be doing something. Norizon was rubbing off on him already.

"Where were you headed?" he asked Lucille.

"To school, him too." She pointed to Neo. "Isn't that where you were going?"

"Um, yes, to school," he said, anxiously. He knew Grelda, and he was wondering if she would recognize him.

• •

"You can walk with us." Neo said and grabbed Barris by the shoulder to pull him with them.

"Oh, I can't wait to graduate and have all these amazing abilities!" Lucille said as they began to hurry to school. "Also to get to places quicker. There's so much to do." She carried her papers against her chest and looked around at other Keepers who were moving in different ways, with different abilities. She stared at one who was floating and with every few blinks of his eyes, the Keeper would bounce and be a little bit farther ahead than he had been.

The gold trim was becoming more prominent in the room, Barris thought. The gold color became brighter and created an intense glow throughout Norizon.

Abruptly, a gust of wind blew through Norizon, which was not uncommon, as the four seasons met at the front door. But the wind was rough. It pushed through Norizon and even pushed the little man in the black and white striped socks, who was walking up and down the staircases in his little "office" in the center of Norizon. He fell and hit the floor with a belly flop.

Barris, Lucille and Neo had to walk sideways against the wind to keep from falling. Barris felt his right foot blow to the left when he lifted it to walk.

Then, as soon as it began, the wind stopped and the prior urgency resumed in the room.

"Well, that was a big one," Neo said.

"Seasons can be unpredictable, so it makes sense that we would have something pop up once in a while,"

Lucille said, as if a blast of wind blowing people sideways was common.

Lucille led the two boys to a square section of white flooring to the side of the hustle and bustle. It was glowing with the gold trim as a border. Barris was grateful that she naturally took charge so he could follow.

The three of them stood on the four-foot by four-foot square, and when they did, four walls slid up, and then closed over the top of them. On the outside the walls were solid white. But from the inside of a Kystra (KIS-STRA), the walls and ceiling were invisible.

Kystras were a way for Keepers to travel in Norizon. Especially the Keepers who hadn't mastered other mobile abilities yet, like flying or blink-bouncing or leaping.

In their Kystra, the three elevated past a few floors and Barris took note of how different each was. One was full of Keepers taking up most of the floor space, all in different solid-colored socks, and different striped socks, and they were tap dancing. In the corner was a pile of their jackets. It reminded Barris of a dance number from *"Singin' in the Rain"* with Gene Kelly and Debbie Reynolds, a movie he saw the year before at the theater. He loved the *"Moses Supposes"* number, where Gene Kelly, the star, tap danced with such high energy, much like what he was witnessing. While the Keepers tapped, the instructor walked around, instructing. "A Keeper must learn to be quick on their feet, and when doing so, be in control."

"Oh to be done with all this hard learning and to then

just dance and maintain," Lucille said to Neo and her new friend, as they passed the dancing Keepers.

They passed another floor after that. "That's the Larix (LAR-ICKS)," Neo said to Barris. The floor of the Larix was covered with pillows and pads of all sorts of sizes and colors. The walls even seemed soft. And the soft surface provided an extraordinary bounce to the leaping Keepers there. One was holding onto their black hat and jumping from padding on the floor to bouncing off the padding on the wall.

"That's where Keepers go to stay physically fit," Neo continued. "To practice their mobile skills. Some are experienced and others are just developing their travel movements. Depends on how many children they have been assigned." The Kystra stopped a few floors higher than the Larix. All four walls melted back into the gold trim border from where they'd come.

When Barris stepped out first, he was on grass. Grass that was three inches high and moving like wind was slowly rolling through it, creating a whooshing sound as it did so.

"You're new here, right?" Lucille asked.

"Yep," Barris answered, going along with that narrative.

Even though Barris was in his dreams, he wasn't in one of his usual dream worlds. He was in dream headquarters, where all dreams of children are monitored. But the spell Grelda performed that night as a favor to me, masked Barris' "humanness" to the Keepers of the past. I wanted him to have the full experience of a Keeper in training.

• •

"I can tell because you don't have the clothes of a Keeper. Look at those shoes...goodness!" Lucille pointed to Barris' brown slippers. "You're lucky you're with us, you have to either have your Keeper shoes, or have a Keeper with you in order to get into Grelda's school."

"What school?" Barris asked while he looked around him. All he saw was the grass that was rolling with the wind and no sign of a school.

"This school," Neo said. He then stepped onto the top of what looked like the stump of a white oak tree. Neo drew a U-shape with his foot.

Suddenly the wind roared and blew the grass toward the tree stump, which rose up as a new tree and began sprouting branches and leaves at the top. The grass was cascading down, waving like the leafy branches of a weeping willow. But the branches and leaves were so thick, you couldn't see through them to the other side. Barris and his new Keeper friends had been pulled inside the tree. The tree grew and twirled and waved with the roaring wind... and then slipped back into the ground. There was nothing but an echo of Barris' voice asking, "What's happening?!"

5

Chapitre Cinq...

"Voila!" Lucille said, beaming at Barris. "This is Grelda's School for Keepers! Welcome! It's a very sacred place that only those seeking to learn can enter."

They were surrounded by nature because witches draw their power from it, so it only makes sense that Grelda's school is a tree...deep underground.

Barris started to sweat as he looked around the school's smooth, glossy walls. The inside of the school resembled wood, but it was sparkling with green and autumn gold. In the center of the school was a floating platform. Stairs ascended either side of it.

The platform had a dark wood floor, covered with rugs. The students' seats were arranged in a U-shape on it. The ceiling was high and the walls of the platform were covered with different sized wooden rectangles, overlapping and touching each other.

Barris saw a similar sense of urgency there as when he stumbled into the front of Norizon, but now, most of the students rushing about had no flying abilities. They were in training and hadn't developed their mobile abilities quite yet. Those that Barris saw flying when he entered Norizon were older Keepers, not young ones learning. Children were playing, as if they were at recess. Barris was amazed, but also confused. He wondered where I, Gracie, was.

"Ye who enters shall seek the wonder of dreams," read an inscription in gold cursive on the front of the floating platform.

"Let's go get a good seat!" Lucille said and grabbed Barris to run up the side staircase.

Neo followed right behind them. On the sparkling walls around them were giant faded murals. It looked like a big battle being played out upon the walls. Barris saw what looked like Keepers painted in the murals, some in mazes, others leaping in the air, showing all the traits of Keepers and situations they could be in.

"This is a place of history and education," Lucille told Barris as they walked up the stairs. "We learn from the mistakes of the past, but don't dwell on them. We move forward knowing better, with clarity."

• •

Grandma Lucy had always been very wise before her years. Oh how I miss our talks...

Lucille ran ahead of Barris and Neo to snag seats. She saw seats in the third to last row, right on the end. She almost ran into another girl, a trainee like herself who had set her eyes on the same seats. Lucille jumped onto the aisle seat and then stretched out on the other two.

"Lucille, it's not a contest," the trainee said to her in utter annoyance.

"Life's a contest, Eleanor," she responded. Grandma Lucy believed that life was a contest, but more a contest with oneself than with others. "Are you trying to the best of your abilities, and are you standing tall at the attempt?" That was what she would always ask herself in her life and most certainly in her Keeper training.

Barris and Neo walked to sit next to Lucille. "Way to move, Luce," Neo said.

"Pfftt," Lucille said, clearly satisfied with herself.

Barris felt out of place. His striped pajamas didn't blend in with what the other trainees wore.

Everyone was taking their seats. But there was no teacher. In front of the chairs was open air above the rugs on the floor. Barris thought they looked like the oriental rugs his mother had in their house. But they had a light, glowing quality about them.

"Is it Grelda who trains you?" Barris asked Neo and Lucille. Not a moment later, a gust of wind swept over the platform. It wasn't as strong as before, but Barris held his hat, just in case.

Out of the rugs, a sparkling ring formed, and it looked like a hula hoop. The ring turned into the bottom of a woman's dress, and then slid up, revealing the body attached. There she was: Grelda! Long purple dress to the floor, and her sunset-colored cape on top. The cape was draped in layers. You couldn't see her feet. And her blonde hair had pink tips and was pulled back over her left shoulder, barely covering her yellow toned shoulder. She had five pencils in her hair and behind her ears, with a pair of tiny silver glasses on the edge of her nose. They were so tiny that Barris couldn't imagine why she needed them. "No one would be able to read out of those! What's the point?" he thought.

Grelda didn't seem to recognize Barris, nor would she. It was her past self and she hadn't met him yet. Also Grelda made sure when she cast the spell that night to have no wrinkles in the flashback, smooth sailing when it came to questions about Barris' presence.

"And who might you be?" Grelda asked Barris after a few moments of being in the classroom. Her gaze directly on him after she scanned the room to mentally take attendance.

"This is Barris, Miss Grelda, he's new." Lucille spoke out.

"I was not informed of your attendance, but it wouldn't be the first time some information has slipped through the cracks here. Very well then, take notes and keep up." Grelda said to Barris. "And for heaven sakes, Lucille, help the poor boy get his trainee uniform."

• •

"Yes ma'am," said Lucille.

So, Barris sat with his "fellow" trainees and borrowed paper and pencil from Neo. He took notes during Grelda's lesson for the day, which was on a board written in chalk:

- Make sure your assigned child feels comfortable with you. Establish connection immediately.

- Dream worlds of sleeping children are not always so lovely; you can encounter terrible things. Navigate with clarity and stillness. Don't overreact.

- You are there to provide lessons in life; make the most of your time.

Barris took his notes, and listened to Grelda's stories of things she had seen other Keepers do, things they had done correctly, and other things not so much. The class was dead silent; the only thing you could hear was Grelda, the sound of chalk writing and her lecture. When she told stories, they would pop up on a projector in black and white, and play out next to her.

"Now, there, down the stairs the Keeper went. Limited in ability due to not many cases being resolved, and limited in the capacity to see what was best for the child. A little girl, whose reality was a solemn one, but her hope remained. What little hope she had, that is." Grelda spoke so sternly and matter of factly.

Barris was looking down at his paper and had just finished writing "establish connection" from the board, when a loud sound interrupted the class. It sounded like someone banged a hammer against a metal wall.

"Miss Grelda! Miss Grelda!" The little man Barris had seen when he first entered Norizon appeared. He was the person who stood in the middle of dream headquarters and acted as a concierge to the world. His name was Helfi (HELF-EY)...and Helfi was always frantic. But Norizon couldn't operate without him.

Helfi ran to Grelda and whispered eagerly in her ear. It was such a loud whisper that you could hear him, but Barris couldn't make out what he was saying.

"Right. Neo, come up here, please," Grelda said, motioning to Neo, who sat nervous and confused. "Post Haste!" Grelda said more sternly.

Neo nervously approached, and all of his classmates sat in silence to watch. This was not a normal occurrence for class to be interrupted. It must have been important.

Grelda bent a little lower to be close to Neo's face. She could communicate inside your mind when she wanted, if it was something she didn't want to say out loud. And this was something she did NOT want to say out loud.

She, however, could not anticipate Neo's reaction, even though in her communication she told him to remain calm.

"He's lost?!" he shouted.

Neo's dad, Nevarre (NEV-ARR), was a known and popular Keeper in Norizon. He was always willing to help fellow Keepers on difficult cases of their assigned children and mentor trainees.

He had ventured out earlier that evening to go dream-Keep for a little boy in Paris, France. And while there in that little boy's slumber, Nevarre had become lost in a broken dream.

• •

6

———

Chapitre Six... (But With a French Accent)

A wail so loud and shattering it penetrated every corner of Norizon, and it came from a small woman gasping.

Neo's mother, Tira (TEE-RA), clenched her chest while she was being comforted by a group of other Keepers in the main area of Norizon. Helfi brought her tissues that were glowing yellow. After Tira dabbed her tears and wiped her face, she let go of the tissues and they floated out and faded away.

"That is something I never want to get," Lucille said quietly to Barris as they watched Neo and his mother. "A broken dream. We all have heard tales of Keepers getting lost in them, but I have never known of one in my lifetime."

Broken dreams are made up of unpleasant things, and

are a Keeper's worst fear when they are assigned a child. They are labyrinths of trouble, often filled with dark weather, heavy winds, and lightning. The children who have broken dreams are those who live in awful circumstances — children who are orphaned, have horrid parents, or a tragic event has happened that forever affects them.

Neo stood next to his mother, holding her arm at the elbow. Oddly, he felt calm. He looked up at the Gari (GAAH-REE), the moon over Norizon at the tip top of the sky. It appeared sometimes when major events happened, and that night it emitted orange light. Neo looked at the Gari and thought of his father.

Flashback to Neo with his father, Nevarre

"Son, we have a great responsibility. Do you know why that is?" Nevarre looked down to Neo. They were sitting on the padding and pillows of the Larix floor. Nevarre was letting his son watch him practice his mobile abilities. The Larix is where Keepers practiced their physicality.

Neo shook his head no."It's because we shape a child's life," Nevarre continued. They both looked at the Gari. "A Keeper's sole job is to ensure that each young human being keeps their childish innocence, and more importantly, their childish enthusiasm."

A Keeper had just hit a milestone — their 100th child. They had assisted in the development of 100 children, guiding them through many dreams each, successfully. And with that milestone, all of Norizon was a party. The Gari peeped out that night, and gold flakes were falling from it like snow, adding to the celebratory atmosphere.

The golden glow from the flakes reflected in young Neo's eyes and he looked up to his father. "I can't wait to reach my 100th child. And then my millionth!"

Nevarre laughed, touseling the top of Neo's hair and then smoothing Neo's ponytail, "That's what I'm talking about. That hope you have right there, it will carry you throughout your life. Hope is what gets you through anything. In the most ordinary day of ordinary days, most humans don't realize it, but even in the smallest task, hope gets them through.

The hope that the grocery will have their desired item, hope that the letter they've been waiting for arrives. Even hope that they are loved.

"Hope is a tiny little molecule that lives in everything we do. Keep that in mind, Neo, and it will serve you well and the children you help. Nothing is impossible when hope is alive."

Nevarre put his arm around his son as they sat amongst the padding and pillows in the Larix, and looked up at the gold snow that fell. Both their purple eyes were illuminated by the celebrations of Norizon.

Fast forward to Neo standing next to his mother in Norizon

Neo looked at the Gari, and then looked at his distraught mother, still crying, but quietly now. "Mom, let's go home, you need to rest. Father will find his way out and be back soon." Tira nodded, dabbed her eyes again and let the tissue fade away. Neo guided his mom away from the crowd of Keepers who had provided solace.

Tira was a well known Keeper in dream headquarters and had many abilities. She was a thin woman with dark skin, a slick black ponytail that matched her son's, and bright blue eye shadow that covered her eyelids, even above her eyebrows. She had purple eyes, like all of the other Keepers, and she wore a dark purple trench coat. She held onto her son and they faded away to where they lived in Norizon. She left behind a trail of floating, glowing tissues that each evaporated after a moment.

Lucille was impressed when she heard her friend comforting his mother. She thought he was very strong in doing so, and also knew that his heart must be very sad.

"What happens when a Keeper is lost?" Barris asked Lucille. Around them were the Keepers, now talking amongst themselves.

"I don't know. None have ever come back to tell us what happens," she said.

"Can't Grelda help? She's a powerful witch after all," he asked eagerly, seeking answers. He looked over at Grelda who was talking to a group of Keepers.

"No. A broken dream is born of a broken heart. The child is so sad, or angry, that nothing seems like a solution to them. And that is something that no magic can help. The fix for that is the child themselves. They have to want peace, want to navigate their lives, and have a curiosity for the future. When it's an extreme case, a Keeper can get swept up and lose their way from the child in their dream world. They can't find their way back and can't find their assigned child to talk to, to talk them through the darkness," Lucille told Barris.

"So what do we do?" Barris questioned.

"We think, and we research and try to figure out ways to rescue them. None have been successful so far. We have no way to contact them…and we go to the Elklis (ELK-LISS)."

"What's that?" Barris wondered aloud while he saw the Keepers of Norizon beginning to resume the duties they had been performing, before being interrupted by the news of poor Nevarre.

Lucille grabbed Barris' hand and pulled. "Come with me!"

Lucille ran so fast past a Keeper that she caused the stack of papers they were carrying to fly out of the Keeper's arms and create a whirlwind of falling pages.

Through a door they went, behind the center circle where Helfi was stationed, and down a winding stone staircase. Lucille was pulling Barris so quickly that as they passed each lantern on the wall, Barris heard the flame flicker and "swoosh."

"This is the Elklis," she said when they stopped.

Barris looked around. It was a perfectly square room with a solid stone floor, and floor to ceiling picture frames. All hung in perfect straight lines and all were touching the frames above, below and to each side. The walls seemed to meet no ceiling — the top was out of sight.

"These are Keepers," Lucille said in a hushed voice, pointing to the images in the frames. "And these are all Keepers who have been lost."

At that very second, what young Lucille — my Grandma Lucy, that is — wasn't aware of was that she herself one day, many years later, would be in a picture frame on those very walls.

• •

7

Chapitre Sept...

You mean none of these Keepers have come back?" Barris asked Lucille with a shiver.

"Not one. No one has figured out how to rescue a Keeper, and once lost for so long, it can drive a Keeper mad," Lucille's gaze traveled across the portraits. "They can't seem to figure a way out after being alone for so long. In dream worlds, time moves slower. It's to give us time with the child. One night in a dream world really is only a few minutes in your reality."

They both looked around the room at the many frames. Too many to count. The atmosphere was solemn, and cold. Barris was shivering, and Lucille was looking glum in the dimly lit space.

"Let's go. We need to check on Neo."

Barris followed Lucille out of the Elklis. He thought about how Lucille was a good friend, wanting to check on her fellow trainee. He thought back on how he left Pevy in the middle of the street, how cruel he had been, and how she must've felt.

Up the winding staircase they went. As they exited, the lanterns that had been lit when they first entered started to dim on their own behind them.

Back on the main floor of Norizon, Helfi was darting around his enclosed busy space. One shrill ring after another vibrated from the many candlestick telephones. A board in front of him flickered with tiny lights. The board was about the size of a theater screen and was the backdrop of Helfi's work area. The lights reminded Barris of Christmas decorations on trees or in people's front yards during the holidays, all different colors.

"What's that?" he asked Lucille.

"That's all of the children's dream worlds that we monitor. The colors let us know when something is wrong. White light means everything is good, and when it starts to change to different colors, we know something is wrong. And that's when we are assigned cases of those children."

Helfi was juggling papers and running from place to place trying to answer candlestick rings and eye the board. A big bulb went dark. No color at all. A curl of black smoke came from the interior of the bulb.

• •

"That's the world that Neo's dad just became lost in. When a dream becomes broken, the color fades out completely and black smoke appears."

As Lucille spoke, Barris looked at the side of Helfi's area and noticed a big board of unlit bulbs.

"That's where the broken dreams are moved to. That board serves as a record for us."

Barris and Lucille walked toward the Kystra to reach a higher floor within the dream headquarters.

The band of floating instruments that were playing when Barris first entered Norizon were still going as if nothing had happened. Business doesn't stop because of one Keeper being lost. There are millions upon millions of other children to take care of.

Once in the Kystra, the walls slid up from the square of gold trim as before and enclosed Barris and Lucille for their journey upward.

"Where does Neo live?" Barris asked.

"Oh, he's not home." Lucille said. "But I know where he is."

"Wouldn't he be home with his mother?"

"Yes, he will be later. I know he brought her home, but Neo likes to process his emotions alone, before he can process them with other people. I think we have given him enough time alone now."

Lucille could always sense where people were and what they were going through. She was an advanced trainee. No Keepers have ever been like her.

• •

The Kystra stopped at a high floor, and the walls melted back down into the gold trim.

They were at the Larix. Upon stepping off the Kystra, they walked onto the padded floor, usually brightly colored. But the lights were dim now, the color wasn't as noticeable. It was as if the Larix had closed and it was after hours. Just patches of light came in from the rest of Norizon.

Neo was sitting on a big blue pillow. It was the one where he sat with his father the night of the Keeper's 100th child celebration not long ago.

Walking up to Neo, Barris let out an awkward sigh. "I'm sorry for the loss of your father, Neo."

"Don't be," Neo said, "Be sorry for our loss, Norizon's... and for all the children that won't be better off because my father won't be there to help them."

What many don't realize, is that loss is a price to pay in life, and no one gets a free ride. The loss of a family member, the loss of what was or used to be, the loss of an idea, even the loss of your favorite hat. Loss is a big part, and can be the part that shapes us the most.

"I just want to believe in dreams again," said Neo. "Why do humans have to be such complicated creatures?" He looked to Lucille for an answer. He was breathing deeply, and tears filled his eyes.

"Everything's complicated, Neo. And then again it's not. It's not just humans. Your father is lost, he isn't gone. And that means that he's still here and hoping like you are that he will return."

• •

Grandma Lucy was always a wordsmith, even at nine years old, at the end of her Keeper training and the beginning of her career. She was gifted at birth to walk through her life knowing that uncomfortable work needed to be done almost every day. Leaning into every situation to address it head on, she always had a matter-of-fact approach, sprinkled with some hope and positivity.

"We will figure out a way to rescue him. Him and all the other lost Keepers. And if we can't, we will figure out a way to prevent one from being lost again."

Neo stood and began to run through the Larix. His arms tucked tightly to his sides, he ran from one end to the other end. He just wanted to feel something, even if it was only tingling and warmth in his legs for a few seconds.

Flashback to the Larix with Neo and Nevarre

"The faster you pump your arms, the faster your legs naturally move with them," Nevarre said to Neo days before, while they jumped and dashed among the colorful padding. Nevarre was able to leap and float about due to all the dreams of children he had monitored for years and years. Neo liked to be with his father while he sharpened his mobile abilities to stay at the top of his game.

Neo ran in circles underneath Nevarre's shadow, trying to keep up. Helfi was walking by the door of the Larix, carrying a huge stack of papers, so tall you couldn't even see his face. As Helfi passed, he saw Neo running aimlessly while looking up to follow his father flying above him. Neo wasn't watching where he was going; the only thing that mattered was staying with Nevarre.

Fast Forward to Lucille, Neo and Barris in the Larix

The orange Gari shined down on the two Keepers in training and their new friend, Barris. Neo ran for a few moments and then stopped, breathing heavily and staring into space.

"Let's get you out of those strange clothes before we go rewrite the history of Keepers," Lucille blurted out to Barris. She was trying to distract Neo and Barris, who both stood in silence like they didn't know what to say or do next.

"Yes, you are wearing strange clothes," Neo said. "Who wears striped pants and a shirt to match?! And don't even get me started on that pack," Neo said, sounding more like himself. Clearly, Lucille's distraction worked.

"This pack right here, my grandfather gave me." Barris felt the smooth leather of his homemade pack. "To always make me feel prepared. He's away right now, I guess you can say that he's lost too. We see him sometimes, but he's not there," Barris looked down and started to show Lucille and Neo the things within his pack. He began to tell his friends about his Papaw Leo.

When Neo heard Barris' story of the origin of the pack, and about Papaw Leo who was now living in a "big white building with other old people in New York," he smiled and grabbed the side of the pack to tighten it for Barris. "Well, we better make sure you don't lose it, eh?"

The three of them walked out of the Larix, Lucille leading the way. Obviously she was going to be leading this "Keeper-Saving" project.

Barris began peppering Lucille with questions about what they were about to do. Neo stopped and looked around the empty room that was full of moments with his father. He appeared lost in past memories.

Neo shook his head to get out of his daze and ran to catch up to Lucille and Barris. He ran so fast that his flat ponytail flew up and blew in the wind with his dash. He bounced from one pillow on the right over to a pillow on the left and bounced right in front of Lucille. "Let's move like we mean to, shall we?"

8

Chapitre Huit...

Barris, Lucille and Neo hopped on the Kystra outside the Larix with speed and on a mission.

"Where are we going?" Barris asked.

"To the Storik (STO-RIK). It's where all the records are kept of Keepers and the history of sleeping children," Lucille replied.

As the walls of the Kystra rose from the gold trim at their feet, Neo's disposition had clearly shifted to one of purpose. He was no longer sad. He had redirected his sadness toward something productive, which is how one can cope with a big change.

Up higher and higher the trio went on the floating platform. Barris felt his stomach do somersaults when the speed quickened.

The air was different at the top of Norizon. It was very still. Particles like green glitter floated in the dim lit atmosphere, sparkling. Not many went to the top and the Kystra had to elevate with all its might to bring them there.

The walls melted down and Barris heard a familiar sound...the chatter of dust mites.

"I forgot how loud their whispers are!" said Barris.

"You've heard them before? Didn't you just get here?" Lucille asked.

"I've read about them." Barris said. "In my Keeper pre-studies." He didn't want to mention the world of Rappa where dust mites were prominent.

"Yup, they're loud little critters, but they can come in handy sometimes," Neo chimed in, recognizing the swarming sound of the chittering dust mites.

"But wait!" Lucille shouted.

Barris and Neo both jolted.

"Let's get you out of your odd clothing so I have something presentable to look at while we work. We have to fix this."

Outside the Storik was a pile of dusty trench coats. They were old and there were many. They were piled so high that the pile was taller than all three of the friends even if they had been standing on each other's shoulders.

"Wear one of these," Lucille said, as she grabbed a gray jacket from the middle of the pile.

"Yuck. I'm not wearing that old thing." Barris sneezed.

"It's better than what you're wearing." Lucille said, sternly.

Lucille tossed the jacket to Barris and when he caught it, a cloud of dust mites erupted from it. Their whispers filled the room, like the sound of a car rushing by.

Barris put on the light gray coat; it was so big it was like a large quilt. He wrapped it around his body and fastened the middle with the attached black belt.

Buckling the belt closed, Barris looked down at his feet. He could see that they were standing on a stone floor, similar to the floor in the Elkris with all the frames of lost Keepers. But it was very dark there. He could make out silhouettes of things, but he couldn't make out what anything was. The Gari seemed to be right on top of them now, but the glow was fading.

"Alright, now that's taken care of, let's get to work," Neo said. He patted Barris on his back and more dust flew off, along with whispers.

The three started to walk into the darkness and as they did, lanterns on the ground and walls slowly lit up showcasing their surroundings.

The lanterns were staggered all along the walls and there were many of them. The light bulbs in green bankers' lamps lit up slowly on tables, highlighting mountains of books on them. The lights were too many to count; Barris thought that the many lights looked like the ones he saw in pictures of all the buildings in New York City at night.

"We will find our answers here," Lucille said. "Here is where all the dreams of children are recorded and those who have been lost in them. What others have tried and plans of rescue that were never executed."

Once the space was fully lit, Barris looked around to take it all in. It was a large room with leather couches, stacks of books everywhere and file cabinets stacked against walls, some on top of other cabinets, where there weren't any lanterns. Some of the file cabinets were open, pages hanging out of them. Open books on the large wooden tables next to them told the stories of Keepers who had sought information before them. It reminded Barris of a very old, crowded full library.

"I don't even know where we would start," Barris said loudly. "It's so much to go through! And I hate reading."

"You start, Barris, by grabbing a book." Lucille said. She walked toward an open file cabinet, peeped inside, moved her fingers through the pages that lived there, and pulled out a stack. "Everything in here is useful, and that's the way to look at it."

"That's right, nothing in here is useless," Neo agreed with her.

Barris let out a deep sigh. He was a little overwhelmed. He walked up to one of the large tables that were covered in books in the middle of the room. All of the books were old with thick leather binding. The pages were yellowed, with worn edges. Neat handwritten notes filled the margins.

Someone had clearly been there before researching the history of broken dreams and lost Keepers. Barris sat down and slid one of the books across the table towards him. It was open to a page with the drawing of a maze, with lightning and clouds above it. He began to read. He held the large book in his arms, holding it closer to his eyes to read it better.

"Try this," Neo said. He picked up a lantern on the floor and put it next to Barris on the table.

"Merci," Barris said, his eyes not leaving the book.

"You're such a sophisticato, newbie," Lucille said. "Mais, excuse moi, I can speak French too." She laughed and started reading the pages she had pulled out of the cabinet. Neo stood next to her to thumb through the paperwork.

• •

Barris was reading the yellowed pages. The words seemed to jump from the pages, alive with a story.

She is but a dark child, born of nothing and doomed to dwell in what that is. When with her, I bring nothing but enthusiasm to push her out of her own way.

As Barris read, he began to feel goosebumps come over him, a sense of pessimism as he read about the broken dreams of a child.

Many will call her an untouchable, but I call her Sophie. It's a beautiful name and she should be addressed as such. Minor progress has occurred, more to hopefully come.

—September 2, 1915 Doxia

Barris reread the entry from the Keeper about Sophie, this time out loud.

"I've heard of that one!" Lucille said. "Doxia was a great Keeper. She would get lost in broken dreams for the smallest moment, but was always able to reconnect with the child and get back to Norizon. Her cases and escapes are legendary here in Norizon."

"What happened to her? What's an untouchable?" Barris asked.

"That case, Sophie, became such a hopeless cause that Doxia got lost one night, not long after that entry and no one's seen her since." Lucille said. "An untouchable is a child who you think will start to develop broken dreams, and you have to let the case and the child go."

"And no other Keeper can go into that child's dreams?" Barris questioned Lucille. He couldn't believe Keepers would give up.

"That's impossible, Barris. Each child's Keeper is assigned to them, as if they were their parents. And because Keepers can't communicate with their assigned child unless they are sleeping, it's hard to escape a lost dream unless the Keeper can reconnect with the child while they sleep. A kid who has really bad broken dreams, well, their mind doesn't entertain such things when they close their eyes at night...dreams that is. Once their heads hit their pillows, they dream of nothing."

Neo let out a sigh, but then cleared his throat, as if catching himself. He wanted to sound more optimistic. "But, that's not the case here. My father was dream-Keeping with a little boy named Toby, and Toby isn't a lost cause. Let's look up Toby's file and see what we can maybe do to help."

Neo approached a stack of papers labeled "*T*."

The letter "*T*" was floating above the stack, being written in cursive, over and over, by an invisible sparkler. Barris hadn't seen that sparkling letter before, but as he looked at it now, a row appeared on both sides of the "*T*" with the rest of the alphabet, being spelled out mid-air as if with a sparkler.

"How do you know what to do when something like this

happens?" Barris asked Lucille.

"What do you mean?"

"It's an awful thing that has happened, and you were there for your friend and gave him hope. And now here we are, finding a solution," Barris said in a lower voice so Neo wouldn't hear.

"Barris, you just do it, you just act, you do or say something, anything," Lucille looked into Barris' eyes. "You put all of your awkward feelings aside and the sadness aside, and you let them know you're there. Ask what they need. But the important thing is to make sure they keep faith. In the worst situation, to have a belief in something, something better or something to help them cope. Even if you can't imagine what that something is.

"When you live a life with no faith, you are doomed to have it ruled by pessimism. And well, nothing good can come of that, for anyone."

"Pessimism?" Barris asked.

"Yeah, when you lose your hope and ability to accept anything on faith, well, you're just like one of those kids in those books. Waking up, believing in nothing, and going to bed dreaming of the same, and then not dreaming at all. And well...who wants to live a life with no dreams? Even when you're not sleeping."

Barris nodded. He turned back to the pages. He was sure they had to have answers.

He licked his finger and turned the page. "Fancy,"

he thought, and then, "Ugh, I'm becoming Bernice now!" crossed his mind next.

The Gari moon above them had slid to the edge of Norizon, about to disappear.

Barris had a feeling in his stomach like he was on a rollercoaster. He looked at Lucille who had climbed to the top of a stack of cabinets against the wall, and was now head first in a drawer, digging through papers. Her legs with green socks flailed in the air, accompanied by her grunts.

He looked at Neo who was desperately trying to find a clue on the child his father was helping, while trying to dream-Keep. "I think I found something!" Neo shouted and held a page in the air.

Lucille popped her head out of the drawer. They both looked to where Barris had been standing.

A pile of papers was drifting slowly to the floor, surrounding the dusty trench coat he'd been wearing, a big brown book on top. Barris was gone.

• •

9

Chapitre Neuf...

"Fiddly deeee, fiddly daaaaa. La la lalala." Mrs. Hart's voice surrounded the walls of Barris' room. He opened his eyes slowly.

He wiggled his tootsies underneath the pillows he had on top of them. "Tootsies" were what Mrs. Hart called feet. Barris could sleep well only if he had pillows on top of his feet. Made him feel all snuggled in his bed.

Barris stretched his arms and sat up to put on his slippers. He sat on the edge of his bed and let his feet dangle for a second, while he reflected on Norizon and what had just happened there. He wondered if Neo's father would be rescued from the broken dream and if Lucille and Neo would find what they were looking for. Also, he wondered where I was. Then he thought of his friend.

"I need to talk to Pevy," he thought. He hopped out of bed and put on his brown slippers and proceeded to walk out of his room down the hall.

The door to Betsy and Betty's room was opened slightly. They were inside, listening to a song on the record player from one of their parents' albums. It was the song from Mr. and Mrs. Hart's wedding, *"Canon"* by a German composer named Johann Pachelbel, a beautiful tune. It was the song playing as Mrs. Hart walked down the aisle.

Betsy had the long white curtains that draped to the floor from their bedroom windows covering her head, acting as a veil. Betty was at her side, tossing feathers in the air that she took from one of her pillows, pretending it was rice. They were both still in their sleeping robes, Betsy in light blue and Betty in light green.

The feathers fell slowly and the giggles from Barris' sisters echoed through the hallways upstairs, with the record playing and Mrs. Hart singing downstairs. Barris thought, "How blissfully ignorant they are."

He knew he had been in the same category as them, as their lives and family dynamic remained unchanged and happy. The day before, he had known nothing but mostly happy families and homes, and he thought all were like his. But he had witnessed a father become lost, separated from his loved ones. And his own good friend Pevy, whose parents were choosing to separate and unhinge Pevy's everyday life.

• •

Barris walked down the staircase in his tall green house, past the pictures of his happy family on the wall. He purposely didn't look at them out of guilt.

I was there too, I had just finished my dream-Keeping night with Bernice Hart, but we will fruit loop to that story later. I got distracted watching Betsy and Betty play "wedding" upstairs. The feathers falling created quite the atmosphere and admittedly I wanted to play, too.

I skedaddled around the twin's door frame, feathers stuck in my red spaghetti hair. I ran past Bernice who was yawning as she opened her bedroom door. I was with Bernice all night and I wanted to check on Barris to see if he had learned anything from his Keeper the night before. He was with Grandma Lucy — Lucille — and her friend Neo in Norizon.

Barris shuffled to the dining room table, not picking up his feet.

"Barris, pick up those feet, Chéri," Mrs. Hart said to him as she squeezed oranges in the kitchen to make juice for the family. She was wearing a bright red knee-length dress. It hugged her waist and poofed out below. She had on a white apron with black polka-dots.

It was Friday morning and the beginning of the end of Spring Break for the children. Mrs. Hart wanted to give them a good breakfast for the start of their fun-filled weekend before they had to return to school again on Monday.

Everything in the Hart's dining room seemed to glow that morning, as the sun beams forced their way in, shining

• •

through the windows. Barris didn't know if it was actually the sun or it was just his outlook that made everything seem different. Everything seemed warmer than usual. But his mother tended to make their house feel that way.

Bernice skipped to the table, "Oh, good morning, Mother."

"Bonjour, Chéri!" Mrs. Hart answered.

"Why are you in such a happy mood?" Barris asked.

I sat in the doorway from the kitchen to the dining room and watched Mrs. Hart stirring the grits on the stove, squeezing an orange into a pitcher, and flipping a pancake on the griddle, seemingly all at once. The kitchen was a stage for Mrs. Hart, and she never missed a show, or an opportunity to draw oohs and aahs from her family.

"Why brother dear, can't I be in a good mood after a dreamy night of sleep?" Bernice said. I was starting to like my newest case, Bernice. She was chipper, but dark sometimes, with a dash of sarcasm thrown Barris' way. And any chance someone else could be sassy to Barris when I couldn't, I'll take it.

"Well isn't that just amazing Bernice. I am so, so, soooo happy for you," he replied.

Betsy and Betty came down the stairs giggling. They had feathers in their hair and Betty twirled when she arrived at the table and landed at her seat.

Barris rolled his eyes at the glorious scene his three sisters were making.

• •

As Ella Fitzgerald sang from the record player, Mr. Hart came down the stairs in his sweater vest and tie.

"Good morning Hart children! How are we today?" he shouted into the dining room, and moved quickly to the kitchen. "And good morning Hart wife! How are thee?" he put his arms around Mrs. Hart's waist while she flipped a pancake, and she put a dot of batter on his nose and kissed his cheek.

Barris laughed when he saw Bernice; she was looking at Betsy and Betty in disgust with the feathers in their hair and them talking about what they wanted their weddings to be like. Bernice was definitely not thinking about her wedding. Or "weddings" as Auntie Taflinda would say, "life is too long to only have one." Bernice never knew what she meant by that. But she planned to find out next summer when she went to go and stay with the Aunties in New York City. She couldn't believe her mother was letting her go.

After Barris laughed, he remembered Pevy and how she needed a friend.

He would talk to her tomorrow morning, after she finished up her last day at Madame Sylvie's today.

10

Le Fin...

Pevy sat, a pencil in her hand. She stared blankly at the paper where she was about to write her name. It was cloudy and cold that morning — at least inside *Madame Sylvie's Charm School for Girls*.

She finished writing her last name, "*Wollendrop.*" Had her mother gotten sick of writing her last name too, she wondered, as she finished the "*p*" in cursive. She was in the third row, sitting in the middle, two girls on either side of her. They were definitely all girls of Madame Sylvie's. They'd appeared every morning looking pristine, drooling on every word Madame Sylvie would say.

Pevy saw her fellow charm school-er, Polly, actually try to inhale a whiff of the Madame's perfume once when she walked by. Pevy was absolutely horrified when she saw that. Polly wanted to be just like Madame.

Pevy was taking her final exam on her final day at the charm school that Friday morning. She dressed for the

occasion with ankle-length white socks, her black Mary Janes she never wore but her mother always begged her to, a long light blue skirt that went down to her ankles, and a white collared shirt tucked in. She slept with her hair in curlers the night before, just like her mother. She was determined to graduate from school…and then to never return.

Oui, vous avez terminé, Miss Wollendrop?" Madame Sylvie asked Pevy if she was done, as Pevy began walking her test to the front of the room and to a white wooden podium where Madame stood. Anastasia sat at a desk in the corner, grading the tests that were turned in.

"I have completed my exam, Madame Sylvie," Pevy said, handing it over.

"Pevania, let's go for a stroll, oui?" Madame said.

"Oui, Madame," she answered.

The two of them walked out of the classroom, down the wide hallways, through the foyer, and up the stairs to go to the top porch.

Out on the upstairs front porch, Madame Sylvie sat on the swing at the top of the school. It was a large hanging wooden bench, with white and light pink cushions decorating it. Madame patted the cushion next to her, gesturing for Pevy to sit.

Pevy was still trying to get a good grade and complete charm school successfully. She crossed her feet while she sat, just as she was taught.

• •

"Pevania, you have done well this week, and you are going to pass. A good report I will deliver to your mother," she said, adjusting her pearl necklaces as if it was her last chance to touch them again. She looked off into the distance. She was wearing a black pencil skirt that day, with black high heels, and a ruffled silk shirt, her usual uniform.

"I want you to know that I know what is going on within your home. Your mother alerted me when you were enrolled."

"Oh," Pevy said, and looked down at the porch floor, embarrassed.

"I want you to know that I am divorced. I was married back in Paris before moving to New Orleans years ago."

Pevy's eyes widened and she looked up at Madame Sylvie, "You were?"

"Oui." She played with a pearl on her necklace and then moved on to the next in line. "You see, Pevania, we live our lives, and rarely do we think that it's about anything other than ourselves. We forget about the way those around us view life."

Pevy felt like a popcorn kernel had popped into her head, "Gee Madame, I never thought of it that way."

"I know, that's why I'm telling you," she said, bluntly. "Your parents have lived lives, lives where you know nothing about what they dream of or want. Just like they will never know every little thing about your life. And while it makes you feel uncomfortable with what your parents are going through, it's not about you. They still love you and will continue to do so. This is about them and what will make them happy. Do you want them to stay together just because that's the way it was? Knowing they will fight, and not be happy?"

"No I suppose not."

"That's correct, Pevania. We all deserve to be in love… many times. That's what I hope for. And what better luck to have? People fall in love, and people fall out of love. You know, when I met my ex-husband I was 18 years old. Years flew by and we grew up, and I realized I wasn't the young girl he fell in love with anymore, and he wasn't the boy I eloped with against my parent's wishes. We are mysterious creatures, we constantly change. And sometimes," Madame bent down to look Pevy in the eyes, "that means choosing to not stay in a marriage where there is no love, nor what you Americans call…'butterflies?'"

"Butterflies?" Pevy asked.

"Oui, the butterflies. When you are so in love with someone, that you are so anxious to see them and time stops…" Madame Sylvie was staring into her past, beyond the porch. She cleared her throat and again looked at Pevy. "When that is gone, and your heart tells you, avec certitude, it will not return, there is no rational reason to stay. Rational to the heart that is. Would you want to stay with someone you weren't in love with anymore?"

"No, I would not."

"Voir, there you go," Madame said. "And if you do find someone that you want to stay with forever, the secret is that you have to think they are the greatest thing in the

• •

world, all the time. I didn't think my ex-husband was the greatest thing in the world anymore. And not just for one day, many of them."

"It's not just that my parents are separating," Pevy said, wanting to cry. "I told my best friend Barris about it, to have someone to talk to, and he got really strange and rode away on his bike."

Madame Sylvie intertwined her multiple pearl necklaces in her fingers. "Your friends will understand, eventually, even if they don't at first. Just give them time, just like you needed time when your parents told you. You are all of ten years old, you're still learning and growing. And to be honest, so am I. So it never stops."

"Can I say Madame Sylvie, I thought you hated me all week!"

"Oh darling girl, I'm just tough because I want all women to be strong and tough when they go out into the world. And I don't hate anyone. Of course, there are some I don't like very much, especially those who have brown on their nose from being up my fanny."

They both laughed. Pevy thought of Polly.

"Let's go and get your charm certificate and then I'll tell you girls the story about a young woman who lost her way, and then found it again underneath a spotlight at the Moulin Rouge."

"Moulin Rouge?" Pevy asked.

"Oui, The Red Mill."

• •

10.2

Le Fin... (Part Deux)

Pevy tied her brown hair into a tight ponytail, and walked out of her bedroom. It was Saturday, and the first day of her Spring Break, since she had been in school all week, and she had nothing to do. She had successfully completed *Madame Sylvie's Charm School for Girls* and left with a new perspective on life and herself.

While she didn't think she'd be taking everything she learned from the charm school with her, like how to sip tea properly — pinky finger extended — she knew she'd need the more candid advice Madame gave her.

Before she walked out of her bedroom, she went to her closet to pet her dog Charlotte. Charlotte was always anxious. She feared loud noises and most people. But she felt safe with Pevy. And she felt safe in Pevy's closet. Pevy had put a large soft pillow on the floor for Charlotte to curl up on. She patted her head, "Bye Charlotte, I love youuuu."

It was a sunny morning in New Orleans and Pevy walked down the hallway to the kitchen. Mrs. Wollendrop was enjoying the morning paper. Mrs. Wollendrop was dressed in a fitted light pink silk robe, with yellow curlers in her hair. She had on lipstick, but no other makeup. Mrs. Wollendrop believed a woman should always feel pretty, and wearing lipstick always did that for her. No matter what else she was doing.

"Good morning, Mother." Pevy said, and tickled her mother's shoulder as she walked past her to open the refrigerator for a glass of milk.

Mrs. Wollendrop froze for a second. She didn't know how to react since her daughter had been so cold to her since the announcement of the separation.

She smiled and turned her head. "Good morning Pevania. Did you sleep well?"

"I did. I thought that I'd go and meet Barris and them for some Saturday fun. It's the end of Spring Break after all," Pevy said.

"Yes dear, I'm aware. You did so well at Madame Sylvie's, you've earned some fun."

. . . .

Mrs. Wollendrop turned back around to her paper. A green glass plate of half-eaten toast sat next to her, butter melting off it.

"That I have, Mother," Pevy said and twirled around the kitchen. She stopped at Mrs. Wollendrop's chair. "I want you to be happy, and I'm sorry for being angry with you."

"Oh Pevania, happiness has many layers, and your father was just one of them for me. But, you will always be at the core of it...and the same goes for your father! We both love you very much," her mother said, reaching for Pevy's hand.

"That I know," Pevy said matter-of-factly. She leaned down and gave her mother a kiss on the cheek. "I'll be home for lunch." She shouted as she ran out the front door and jumped on her bicycle.

Mrs. Wollendrop stared at the front door. She appeared to get lost in thought, and a faint smile appeared on her face. After a moment, she fluffed her newspaper and adjusted her eyes back to the local news.

Off on her bicycle Pevy went. Wearing her dark green capris, Mary Janes (she had come to like them after a week of wearing them), and white tee shirt. Her ponytail swayed behind her with each pedal.

She felt different on that day. A sense of peace with her ten-year-old life. She thought about what the layers of her happiness would look like moving forward in time.

• •

She pulled up to the Hart residence. Barris was outside; so was Bernice, sitting on the porch steps reading a book.

Barris was bouncing a ball.

"Hiya!" Barris said, happy to see his friend. "Aren't you so glad you're done with that dreadful school?!"

"Eh, it wasn't so bad," Pevy said.

"Are you a 'charmed girl' now?" Barris asked.

"I'll charm you into next week if you don't quit it," she said.

"Golly, I am teasing. But, Pevy...I, um...Well I'm just..." Barris stopped bouncing the ball. "I do want to say I'm sorry for running off the other day, I —"

Pevy cut him off. "It's fine. I get it, it's weird."

"No. It's not fine. I'm your friend, and I didn't behave much like one when you tried to talk to me. I've just never heard of anyone's parents getting divorced before," Barris said.

"Ha, ya know, me neither," said Pevy.

"Well, whatever it is, things that I know and things I don't, I'm here for ya. Just, you know, let me know what you need."

"Today, what I need from you, Barris Hart, is a day of fun. I've been a proper girl all week and I need to not be today."

"Lucky for you, I know two other people who are looking for the same thing today. Let's go get crazy! Oh, and get them, first of course. I'm talking about Dean and Glenda," Barris said. He felt tongue-tied.

"I know who you were referring to," Pevy said.

• •

"Referring to? Wow, you are all proper now that you're charmed!" Barris shouted as he grabbed his bicycle handlebars and jumped on.

Pevy pumped her pedals to catch up to Barris, "I'll show you charmed, Barris!"

I stood in front of the Hart house. I stared at the tall staircase that went up the middle of the large green home. Bernice sat right in the middle, with her back on one post, legs stretched across to the other.

She licked her finger to flick to the next page. She looked at her brother and his friend and shook her head.

I was enjoying getting to know Bernice Hart. She was so different, and her mind was always going places.

I took the last bite of my beignet. The crunchy treat felt like a morning reward to myself after dream-Keeping all night. "My new routine!" I told everyone back in Norizon. Each Keeper had their own routine after monitoring sleeping children all night, and mine had become a crunchy beignet.

I walked up the staircase to read over Bernice's shoulder, licking the sugar from my fingers. She was reading *After the Funeral*, by Agatha Christie, a great author known for her detective novels. Oh, how smart and ahead of her years was Bernice! She was skipping a grade and would be joining Barris's class. I was so excited to be assigned to her as my newest case. Barris wouldn't be needing me anymore. He had just turned ten a couple of months earlier and he would do well in his life with the dreams we had traveled through together.

• •

And just then, in my excitement to explore the dream worlds of Bernice Hart and to see what help she would need navigating, I remembered what young Grandma Lucy said to Barris in Norizon. Life isn't just about us.

Author

Brandt Ricca is a D.C.-based entrepreneur. Having a writing background and a family history of owning a newspaper, telling stories has always been at the forefront of Brandt's mindset.

Creating a narrative is a must for Brandt, who always wants to convey a message with events or imagery through his branding agency, Nora Lee by Brandt Ricca.

Brandt was born in Baton Rouge, Louisiana, and loves the Southern culture and creative atmosphere of New Orleans, which inspired the setting for the life of Barris Hart.

illustrator

Matt **Miller** is a designer and artist that bounces back and forth from D.C. and Florida. For as long as he can remember, Matt has had a passion for expressing his ideas and creativity in drawings and paintings. His artistic background and love for interior design and architecture are the foundation for his interior design and rendering business, Perspective.

With a soft spot for historic architecture of the American South, and gathering inspiration from his own vivid dreams, he felt he was the perfect fit for illustrating the world of the Barris Books series.

www.ingramcontent.com/pod-product-compliance
Lightning Source LLC
Chambersburg PA
CBHW040827120726
48005CB00012B/1533